Mousekin's Christmas Eve

Mousekin's Christmas Eve

story and pictures by EDNA MILLER

PRENTICE-HALL, Inc., Englewood Cliffs, N. J.

Library of Congress Catalog Card
Number: 65-25244

Printed in the United States of America

ISBN 0-13-604447-6 (pbk.)
ISBN 0-13-604454-9

The house was empty.
Mousekin was sure of that.
The carpet that had covered the floor
was gone.
The great stuffed chair
that had stood by the fire
was gone.
The old dog, too tired to care
if Mousekin scurried near him in the night,
was gone.

It had been a happy home
with crumbs to be found after dark and
cotton to be pulled from the great stuffed chair.
Now Mousekin was alone.
He rap-a-tap-tapped his tiny paw
on the bare boards
and the sound echoed from room to room.
Nothing else stirred in the empty house.

Mousekin climbed to the windowsill.
He stretched his slender body to peer
above the ribbon of frost
that twinkled on the windowpane.
The moon cast the long shadows of bare trees.
The wind made them dance on the newly fallen snow.

It was a bright night
and not too safe for a
whitefoot mouse to
venture out.
But Mousekin knew he
must find another home
that night.

He scurried to the floor again
and hurried to a chink near the hearth.
Not looking back, he jumped through
a small opening
and onto the old wooden beams
that led to the world outside.

The wind and cold surprised the little mouse.
With his ears flattened back
and his whiskers pressed close
he hurried through the snow.

Sometimes he ran lightly across
the top of the drifts and when
he heard a sound that worried
him he would tunnel beneath
the snow until all danger passed.

All the world had turned to ghostly white.
A snowshoe hare leaped high across Mousekin's path
and raced to his home in the underbrush.

A willow grouse, more startled than
Mousekin by the hare's sudden leap, flew
from its cover—beating its strong wings
against the frosty air. A snowy owl
hooted from the lonely woods.

Mousekin shivered as he sensed
the danger all about him.
The moonlight and the shadows
played fearful tricks. Was that
a small hemlock bent with snow?
Or was it a weasel in its
winter-white coat waiting and
hiding? Mousekin's heart beat
faster as he hurried on
through the night.

It was when he had stopped for a moment
to catch his breath and warm his toes
beneath his fur
that Mousekin first saw the great blue circle of light.

It covered him and it colored him.
He jumped aside with a start.

In jumping, he found himself
in a circle of bright red.

Then yellow and green surrounded him.
Lavender and gold glistened on the snow.
The white world had vanished
and there was color all about him.

Looking up, Mousekin saw a great house. There was laughter and music inside and a warm light shone from every window.

He hurried to the window ledge
and huddled near its opened warmth
until the music and the laughter stopped,
and one by one the lights went out
in the happy house.

As mice have a way of knowing
just where a mouse-size doorway
can be found,
it wasn't very long before
Mousekin made his way into
a large warm room.

Before him stood a great
pine tree. Mousekin had
never seen such a tree in
the forest. It was decked
in long shimmering icicles
and great globes of many
colors that gleamed
from every branch.

With a little hop Mousekin jumped into its branches. The icicles danced and brushed the balls of color and made a tinkling sound.

As he turned to explore a little farther
he saw a sight that made him jump.
There on the tree
was the strangest mouse
that Mousekin had ever seen.

With a squeak he raced to the very top of the tree. He sat and waited to make certain all was safe—then carefully, not to disturb a single thing that hung on the lovely tree, he made his way down to the underbranches.

Beneath the tree were
bits of cookies, nuts
and crumbs and more
good things to eat
than Mousekin had
ever tasted before.

It was when he had stopped, for a moment,
to clean his silken coat
that Mousekin turned and saw . . .

the crêche in bright moonlight.
The stable had a steep thatched roof.
Inside, hand-carved wooden people kneeled
and there were animal figures with bent
knees, too.

Softly sleeping in the rude manger
lay a tiny baby.

Peace and quiet filled the little mouse.
He felt safe at last
from the great ghostly world outside.

About the Crêche Figures

The hand-carved crêche figures from which Mrs. Miller
sketched belong to the Robert Bacon Memorial
Children's Library in Westbury, Long Island.
They were made available to the artist by
Miss Elizabeth Miller, Librarian.

The figures were carved in the small village of
Oberammergau, in the Bavarian Alps, by an artisan
whose father and grandfather were also wood-carvers.

In 1663, the people of Oberammergau took a vow to
perform a Passion Play—if they were spared from
a raging plague. Now, every tenth summer,
the Oberammergau wood-carvers lay aside
their tools to act in a Passion Play.

Anton Lang, who carved and painted the figures
Mrs. Miller sketched is world-famous for his portrayal
of the role of Christ in the Oberammergau Passion Play.